Pimp in the Pulpit

Thomas Leslie McRae

A publication of

Eber & Wein Publishing

Pennsylvania

Pimp in the Pulpit

Copyright © 2016 by Thomas Leslie McRae

All rights reserved under the International and Pan-American copyright conventions. No part of this book may be reproduced, stored in a retrieval system, or transmitted in any form, electronic, mechanical, or by other means, without written permission of the author.

Library of Congress
Cataloging in Publication Data

ISBN 978-1-60880-560-0

Proudly manufactured in the United States of America by

Eber & Wein Publishing
Pennsylvania

I dedicate this book to God. Thank You, Father, for opening my eyes and allowing me to see what my heart couldn't believe. Because of You, God, I'm not that insecure little boy I once was. So thank You, Father, for guiding my heart to a new beginning and shining Your light so I can prosper with an open mind and a rejuvenated soul.

The Disclaimer

This book is based on personal experiences but not all facts. Most of this book is a combination of truth, wishful thinking, and some imagination, but one thing is for certain—everyone can relate to this book because it's all about family, jealousy, greed, and selfishness. Many of us can relate to these traits—some better than others. So sit back and relax, and please enjoy while I take you on a journey filled with emotions and possible redemption.

Acknowledgements

First and foremost, I want to thank and acknowledge our Lord and Savior for being my most consistent and all-around loving supporter. Thank You, God, for being a huge inspiration because without You none of this would be possible.

To my mother, Mrs. Sylvia A. McRae, I love you and appreciate everything you have done and continue to do. May you always stay blessed and prosper through God.

To my father, Mr. Marshall Edward McRae Sr., thank you for financially supporting me and teaching me lifelong lessons.

To Mrs. Virginia Bell, thank you for loving me when I didn't feel loved. You're my guardian angel and spiritual kin.

To Ronald Spencer, thank you for supporting me and being a genuine, true friend. I'm always in your debt because your kindness and virtue are your greatest assets.

To Ronald Brown, thank you for being a huge supporter and all-around true friend. Your heart is why your mother's legacy will always flourish and never die.

To Earl Devere, thank you for all your words of encouragement and love. I pray you are happy and highly blessed.

To Beverly Weathers, I love you so much. You're the sweetest person I know, and I hope our friendship lasts a lifetime and beyond.

To Eucharia Njoku, I pray you now find peace and spiritual harmony after your husband's passing; know you're loved in more ways than one.

To Jordan Ashby, I pray you are happy because no one deserves it more than you. Best of luck in everything you do and so much more.

To Mrs. Patricia May, thank you for all the positive thoughts and genuine love—the feeling is mutual because your heart is God's reflection.

To Islam Martin, thank you, brother, for being honest and always straightforward. You're a good man and an inspiration to all, especially to me.

Chapter One
Planning the Party

Cleopatra Ebony Goddess Jones was lying in her bed playing solitaire when her cell phone started to ring. She chose to ignore it because she didn't feel like answering the phone; it was her no-good mother Lillian McBride, aka Lucifer.

Lucifer was so furious that Cleopatra didn't answer her call, she left a very provocative and crude message that went like this: *Cleopatra, Cleopatra, it's your mother on the God damn phone. Answer the phone when someone is trying to reach your snotty cute ass. It's Mommy, your mother—answer the phone, bitch! You only have one mother—answer the phone! It makes no damn sense no one can reach you. It's not like you work or have small kids to raise. Answer the phone you stuck-up bitch because I need to speak with you immediately!*

Cleopatra was so tickled by Lucifer's voicemail she couldn't wait to call her youngest son Eddie Jones and tell him what had just happened. Eddie was at work, but it was a slow night, so when his mother called him he was happy to hear from her. Once she told him what had happened neither one of them could restrain themselves from laughing hard and loudly.

You see, Cleopatra and Edward already knew why Lillian McBride had called them—she was trying to find out if the Jones family was going to attend her ninety-fifth birthday party and, more importantly, how much money they were giving to contribute to the party.

You see, Cleopatra Ebony Goddess Jones and her other two older siblings were approached by their younger sister Viola McBride about throwing Lucifer a huge event for the occasion, even though Viola was the only one capable of handling such an event and financial burden. She, however, tried to play on everyone's sympathy and was able to get her other two siblings Minister Tierra Joy and Tony McBride to commit themselves to this party for Lillian, their rotten-to-the-core mother.

As a result, Viola decided to let her big sister, Minister Tierra Joy, take over the party planning, and, as usual, it didn't take long for Tierra to turn any family event into a hot, ghetto mess. The first thing she did was go straight into pimp mode and start hustling Viola and Tony out of their hard-earned money, which, to be honest, is typical, standard behavior when you are a pimp in the pulpit. She asked both Viola and Tony for a thousand dollars each because she needed sufficient funds to give their mother a wonderful party.

Before anybody decided to agree with anything, Viola told her brother to ask Cleopatra if she would reconsider participating in the party festivities. Tony didn't hesitate to refuse his baby sister's request. In fact, he even told Viola that he wasn't going to bother Cleopatra because she made it very clear that she wasn't going to give them one damn dime for this party, and she wasn't going to waste her money feeding and entertaining any of those ungrateful, selfish, good-for-nothing bitches.

As a result, the trio decided to work things out among themselves. Tony gave Tierra three hundred dollars and also agreed to cook some turkey wings, chicken wings, and some salmon, while Viola was foolish enough to give Tierra five hundred dollars because she was told that the money was needed right away so Tierra could book the facility and have a secure place to throw this once-in-a-lifetime event.

Viola told Tierra to send her husband Minister Lucas Joy to pick up the money—and before Viola could get off the phone, she already heard a hard knock on her door. Sure enough, it was Minister Lucas Joy eagerly waiting for Viola to open the door and give him the money his wife and he so desperately sought.

Once Lucas got the money, he ran to his car and drove off like he had lost his cotton-picking mind. However, instead of going to the facility in Brooklyn, NY to make the down payment, he went straight home to get his wife and then headed to the highway so they could make their way to their spiritual retreat in Atlanta, GA with Viola's money and self-respect.

Chapter Two
The Unannounced Return

Viola McBride went almost ten days without hearing from Tierra and her husband, but fortunately her brother Tony gave her a courtesy call and informed her that both Tierra and Lucas had finally arrived back to New York City.

Viola was disgusted to learn that they came back two hundred dollars short of the money she gave them for the party. Tony explained to Viola how Tierra was able to negotiate for the center and got it at a lower price, but Viola still has yet to see any form of receipt to verify any payment at all, leaving her feeling like her sister financially raped her yet again.

Meanwhile Eddie Jones was at his job doing routine maintenance work with his co-worker Owen Star when he ran into his grandmother's old friend Miss Bailey, who immediately asked Eddie if he and the Jones family were going to his grandmother Lillian McBride's birthday party.

Eddie looks Miss Bailey in her eyes and says in a firm tone of voice, "I didn't know the party was still on. We haven't heard nothing from anyone about anything."

Miss Bailey tells him his aunt, Minister Tierra Joy, brought her and several members of his grandmother's senior citizen home an invitation and that the party was on Saturday starting at 5:00 PM and ending at 1:00 AM exactly. Then she tells Eddie they should come and not worry about an invite, but he cuts her off at mid sentence and tells her he doesn't go to anything his Aunt Tierra is having. This way she has no excuse for coming to his events and parties, especially since she has a bad habit of bringing nothing and trying to pack and take everything with her.

Plus, her husband and their daughter Princess both like to eat up other people's food like they are about to be sentenced to death and placed in the electric chair for execution. Edward also informs Miss Bailey how he doesn't appreciate Aunt Tierra always bringing extra mouths to feed and trying to always get over on his mother Cleopatra and her kind, genuine nature.

He tells Miss Bailey that all of his mother's siblings and even her own mother are spiteful, mean-spirited, hateful, evil individuals who should all be ashamed of their selfish ways and who need to make peace with God since it's a known fact that He isn't pleased with any of those heathens.

Miss Bailey was so shaken up by Edward's comments that she left him and his partner to complete their work. Meanwhile, she made several phone calls on her cordless phone.

After Edward and his partner Owen Star were done with their task, they proceeded to make their way back to the truck when Edward receives a phone call from his mother. Apparently his chat made an impression on Miss Bailey because she informed Lillian that the Jones family was a potential no-show to her party because Tierra stole the funds from Viola, pocketed most of the money, and is back to her old tricks. At least that's what she got from the conversation with Edward Jones.

How Cleopatra found this out was because Lillian contacted Viola, and Viola repeated everything back to Cleopatra. Edward spoke with his mother from the time he entered the van until he and his partner returned back to the base.

Apparently Tierra was angry that word was spreading like forest fire about how she ripped off her baby sister yet again, but instead of Tierra getting her act together and starting to act like the so-called godly woman she portends to be, she proceeded to do her typical nickel and diming in hopes of throwing her mother a big birthday bash, which eventually turned into a piss-poor, sorry excuse for a birthday party and one of the trashiest events ever thrown in history. Considering Tierra's track record, that really is saying something.

Chapter Three
The Family Gathering

Eddie was riding in the car with his parents Cleopatra and Marcus Sr. and older brother Marcus Jr. The family spent the day together and was enjoying each other's company while taking care of some business when Cleopatra received a phone call from Roscoe McBride, her nephew from Haiti.

Now what was interesting about the call is that the Jones family hadn't seen or heard from Roscoe McBride since he was ten years old when his father Tony pretty much abandoned him on the Jones' family doorstep so he didn't have to spend any time or money on him. But despite all the countless, selfish acts Tony McBride has committed against Cleopatra and her family, she never once mistreated Tony or his son Roscoe.

Needless to say, she was caught off-guard by his call since they haven't spoken in years. Roscoe wanted to know if he could hang with the Jones family because he and several members of the family came up to New York City to attend Lillian's ninety-fifth birthday party. He was at the Holiday

Inn Hotel but unable to do too much moving around; he got his ass whipped when he got caught with some other young man's old bitch. The young man flew into a rage when he caught Roscoe in bed, banging out his seasoned old veteran pussy a few months back.

Cleopatra told Roscoe she had some more things to do but she would see him later on tonight. She then asked him if his father knew he was in town. Roscoe answered yes and said he spoke to Tony earlier that day and asked him to come by and see him so they could do some catching up. But as usual, Tony gave a lame excuse and basically blew Roscoe off so he could run the streets and act like the unfit father he really was.

Cleopatra gets off the phone with Roscoe and immediately calls her bitch of a mother because she knew exactly who it was that gave Roscoe her cell phone number. Lillian was notorious for giving out other people's personal information without getting authorization or permission. Cleopatra calls and asks her straight up why she gave Roscoe McBride her number, stating she has a bad habit of giving out her number to anybody and everybody. Lillian proceeded to lie and said she thought Roscoe had her number, but before she could finish that lie, Cleopatra just hung up the phone; she didn't want to hear that trifling whore of a mother tell any more lies and bullshit stories.

After everything was completed, Edward, Marcus Jr., and their mother proceeded to take Marcus Sr. to work, and from there decided to make a detour to see the family members at the Holiday Inn Hotel. Once they arrived at the hotel, Cleopatra was greeted with a big old bear hug by her sweet and always-so-lovable cousin, Marsha Smith, aka Marvelous Marsha. It was a real treat for the Jones family to see everyone, especially Marsha Smith who was one of Cleopatra's favorites along with Eddie Jones.

But considering Marcus Jr. hadn't seen any of his family in a much longer time, this was especially very exciting for him. And to make this moment perfect, the Jones family finally got a chance to see their baby cousin Mia Smith, aka Adorable Angel.

Everyone was speaking and interacting like they never lost touch, and for a moment Edward forgot about how his aunt had caused so much confusion and drama with the family along with Lyla Fraud, her partner-in-crime cousin from Glen Clove, TX.

Now to be honest, Edward has had a beef with his aunt and his cousin Lyla from Texas for quite some time; it all started when the Jones family got sick and tired of Tierra Joy, her husband Lucas, and their daughter Princess constantly abusing their generosity and kindness, and as a result the Jones family decided to kick the Joy family out of any family gatherings they sponsored with their own money.

So when Edward and Cleopatra decided to throw Marcus Jones Sr. a retirement party, they couldn't comprehend how Lyla and Tierra were able to get in the mix because neither of them was invited and neither of them was sent an invitation. Both, however, intervened with the arrangements and managed to invite sixty family members from down south, forty-six of them being from Glen Clove, TX.

The sad fact of the matter is Minister Tierra Joy and Lyla are two of the biggest shit-starters and greatest hustlers of all time, especially Tierra who will always be known and remembered for her greed and ungodly-like actions.

Edward, his brother Marcus, and their mother were talking to their cousin Marsha Smith and her baby girl Mia for almost a half hour when Marsha finally suggested to take the Jones family back to their room. Once they arrived to their destination they found themselves being smothered by several of their Glen Clove, TX, family members, but the main ones who stood out to Edward were his two cousins Luther Fraud and Raymond Fraud.

Now Luther was in the navy for a large portion of both Edward's and Marcus Jr.'s lives, so they just started to establish some kind of a relationship with him. Both young men, however, have a genuine respect for their cousin Luther and his honesty, especially since he and their cousin Marsha Smith are the only southern family members who aren't content on kissing Minister Tierra Joy's ass like she's the queen of England.

Raymond Fraud is Edward's favorite, even though he followed Tierra in the hopes of trying to highjack his father's retirement party along with his baby sister Lyla who, by herself, is a snake in the grass.

While Edward and Marcus Jr. spoke with Luther and Raymond, a rather tall, unfamiliar gentleman enters the room. He doesn't hesitate to give Cleopatra a big hug and a kiss on the cheek. By the time the gentleman makes his way to Edward and Marcus, their cousin Marsha Smith informs the boys that they were looking at her brother and their cousin as well, Phillip Smith.

After everyone was formally reintroduced and spent sufficient time with each other, the family all decided to go back downstairs to see if the rest of the family was done listening to Minister Tierra Joy preach her sermon in the reserved ballroom on the lobby floor.

Cleopatra was happy to see one of her other favorite cousins from Glen Clove, TX, Gina Fraud. When Gina saw Cleopatra, she screamed so loud with excitement it made the Jones brothers smile with a passion so bright it could have lit up the stars from the dark clouds. The boys gave their hugs and kisses to Cousin Gina and after a long conversation in the lobby, Gina decided to kidnap Cleopatra and the boys and take them upstairs to her room.

In her room, they spoke about many things among themselves and along with Gina Fraud's girlfriend from Glen Clove, TX, Miss Helen Lowe. Helen Lowe felt the need to pursue Marcus Jones Jr. even though it was clearly not approved by Cleopatra. But fortunately Gina Fraud had the good sense to shut her friend down before anything serious came out of a no-win situation for Helen Lowe.

Cleopatra and the boys were ready to go, so Gina walked them down to the elevator. They said their goodbyes and made their way to the lobby to give the other family members their hugs and kisses before leaving to pick up Marcus Jones Sr. from work.

Ironically though, Edward couldn't help but think how they saw everybody in the family—including Minister Tierra Joy, daughter Princess Joy, and her stepdaughter Jackie Joy—and no one bothered to inform Minister Tierra Joy that her sister and nephews were in the facility mainly because everyone, including Jackie Joy and Princess Joy, knew that the Jones family was overall sick of Tierra and her bitch of a mother Lillian.

The Jones family made their way out of the Holiday Inn Hotel and made great timing in picking up Marcus Jones Sr. from his job. From there the entire Jones family made it back home safe and sound and all Edward, Cleopatra, and Marcus Jr. could do was talk about their outing with the family and whether or not they were going to attend the ninety-fifth birthday bash of Lillian McBride.

Chapter Four
It's Party Time

As Marcus Jones Sr. made his way out the door, he woke Cleopatra to tell her he was leaving for work and to ask her if she reconsidered going to Lillian McBride's ninety-fifth birthday party. When she told her husband no, he became annoyed and disgusted, which is a mystery to Edward Jones. Why was his father so hell bent on going to or participating in a party for a woman who has treated him and his wife like a couple of lap dogs? Why in God's name would he want to support anyone so cold and callous towards him and his family? Marcus Jones Sr. decided to tell his wife that the only reason why he's so pushy on the subject matter about her family is because he doesn't speak to any of his; plus, both of his parents were dead.

Cleopatra's response was, "I can see you being so sentimental to both of your parents—they both loved you and showed you love while they were here. All mine ever did was lie, cheat, and steal from me my whole life, and I refuse to let history repeat itself with our own kids."

Marcus Jones Sr. storms out of the room with a real funky attitude demanding Edward help him bring some stuff down to the car. While the father and son were riding the elevator down to the lobby, Marcus Sr. looks at his son and says, "Your mother is being ridiculous. Things aren't as bad as they were before. Besides, her family has finally warmed up to me, and I feel like I'm a part of this family now."

Edward loses his cool and goes off on his father. "What the fuck do you mean you finally feel like a part of this family? These ungrateful, self-hating bitches left us high and dry during the hurricane Sandy disaster. Lillian knew y'all had no heat or hot water and took in two total strangers instead of taking you in. As a matter of fact, the only time she even offered to take you and Mommy in was when she spoke with someone in her neighborhood and they told her to see if she could get y'all to tie up your deep freezer on the roof of the car, drive across the bridge and try to bypass the national guard, and bring her all your fresh fish from Boston we caught along with all the other food we had. You honestly can't be this foolish."

Marcus Jones Sr. replied, "What about your aunt Minister Tierra Joy? She offered to take us in before the storm hit and your mother refused her offer."

Edward Jones replied, "Yes, first of all we didn't know how bad the storm was going to be and furthermore you know damn well if we would have gone there Tierra and her family would have been in our pockets for so long we wouldn't even have had enough money to buy our own food let alone pay any of our bills." Edward looks his father in the eye and says, "Name one time Tierra did anything for us without having some kind of hidden agenda behind her actions. Just because she's a minister doesn't mean she isn't a pimp in the pulpit."

Marcus Jones Sr. just shook his head, went straight to the car, and drove off like a madman. Edward couldn't help but think to himself, *Man my dad is really a lost soul. How can you love those who hate you and resent the ones who will always love you?*

Once Edward made his way back in the apartment, his mother called him in her room so she could tell him how Aunt Viola decided she wasn't going to Lillian McBride's birthday party neither and that she could kick herself for allowing Tierra full control of the party event.

As it turns out, Viola had paid for a young man to come to the event and set up his catering service, but Tierra refused to allow the caterer to come in and perform his duties. In fact, she, Lyla, and some of Tierra's church family bum-rushed the young man at the front door, denied him entry, took the food, and told him they would take care of everything, that he wasn't needed to serve the food. They said since Viola wasn't there at the event, he would have to go back to her place and receive the rest of his money. Then the holy rollers slammed the door in the poor young man's face.

Edward was about to say something but Cleopatra told him to wait, there's more to the story. Apparently several family members called Viola and informed her of how several people came up to the podium to speak about Lillian McBride and how much she gave them and their kids, but the person who stood out the most was Tony McBride, childhood friend Vermin Phony, his wife Toni Phony, and their two boys King Phony and his little brother Kyle Phony. Truth be told, Lillian was more of a mother to her godson Vermin Phony and a much better grandmother to his boys than she ever was to Cleopatra's sons.

People at the party were so upset that the Jones family was a no-show. Edward couldn't understand how these same individuals—for whom Lillian McBride did so much, who in fact did nothing for her or very little—are now mad because the Jones family refused to allow her or the people she loves to continue to get over and use them.

Viola also received word that damn nearly everyone in the family from Glen Clove, TX, tried to eat all the food like a pack of wild dogs, but Tony McBride's childhood friend Vermin Phony, his wife Toni Phony, and their two boys weren't about to be outdone. To make matters worse, when you throw into the mix Tierra's husband and daughter, you have a party no one can speak of without being embarrassed and ashamed, seeing how several of these people couldn't hold their liquor nor their greedy, outrageously ridiculous appetites.

But here's the real kicker—apparently an uninvited guest named Ray Ray busted up in there with six more greedy mouths with no card or gifts, just greedy mouths, and he just kept on dancing and eating like he never had a meal in his life. One would think it was literally going to be his last supper.

Lyla Fraud was in the kitchen stealing the food, packing it up, and putting it in her pocketbook like it was a free soup kitchen. Tony McBride's girlfriend Miss Daisy Lowe was eating like a jackass mixing her wine and soda together like she never had anything to drink. To make matters worse, she was banging on the table hollering and screaming that she wanted some cake even though it wasn't time to serve the birthday cake. Tony had to stop her from banging on the table by saying, "Hey, bitch, what the hell are you doing? You don't bang on no goddamn table like you never had cake before!" Miss Daisy Lowe was so mad she walked away from the table and sat quietly by herself next to some lovely crystal decorations, other high-priced items, and some glasses. All of a sudden there was a loud crash. When everyone looked up they found Daisy standing near the rubble and looking over the shattered glass with a smile on her face and no sense of remorse for her actions.

Before anyone said anything, Minister Tierra Joy jumped up from her seat and started to curse out Daisy Lowe. "Daisy, Daisy, Daisy Lowe, what the fuck is wrong with your sorry, good-for-nothing stale, stinking, rotten, corroded-ass pussy? Where the fuck do you get off destroying my mother's decorations and trying to ruin her golden birthday? Bitch if I was you, I would have a seat and don't say nor do shit without my permission you nasty, stinking whore."

Well, needless to say, the party was over at that point because Daisy Lowe was literally on the verge of getting her ass whipped by damn near the whole entire family, and as a result the party got shut down. That's how Viola finished the story.

Chapter Five
The John Hall Dilemma

As Edward Jones enters the maintenance shop at his job, he finds his former partner and coworker John Hall sitting down on the bench waiting to speak with him. Apparently John and his girlfriend Sophia had finally decided to take their relationship to the next level, and as a result he lost his wife of over twenty-one years, plus a third of his profits and personal assets. But that was the least of John Hall's issues because Sophia was without a doubt the biggest mistake of John Hall's life, and he would explain why.

"Brother," Edward Jones says, "John Hall, it's been too long. You look good! How is everything and everyone, my friend? Edward looks John in the face and tells him to speak his business and not waste his time with trivia bullshit.

"Okay, my brother," says John Hall. "I have a situation. I left my wife for Sophia Cruz, and she is literally bleeding me dry financially and emotionally. I can't speak to my family nor my friends because they all have pretty much disowned me. I know we didn't part on good terms, but I'm desperate and really need some spiritual and emotional guidance." John Hall proceeds with his story.

"Sophia Cruz and I moved in together after three years in a relationship and all she has done is live off of me and waste my time. I'm virtually broke and penniless. Plus, she has me stressed out to the fullest. One night in bed she slapped the taste buds out of my mouth. I immediately woke up and found her standing over me with a butcher knife trying to kill me while screaming, 'You're not giving any other bitch my dick anymore because this dick belongs to me and no other bitch, you whoremonger motherfucker.' I was able to calm her down and eventually we went to sleep, but the morning came and she began to fight with me about not doing enough for her and with her. I told her I was almost tapped out financially, but she refused to hear anything I had to say. So in a moment of weakness, I decided to book us both on a seven-day cruise. When we went she did nothing but show her ass and act like a goddamn fool.

"Just when I thought I was down for the count, my mother and little sister Sasha call me out of the blue. I open up completely to them, explaining my entire situation. My mother told me to come home after I was done taking care of my business because she was going to help me with my situation and get my life back on track. What I didn't know was my mother called Sophia Cruz that Thursday night and informed her that five cars full of our family members were coming up here to New York City, and that the men were staying in that place, and we would see her Friday morning at ten to clean up my apartment.

"Once I got to my mother's place I went into a deep coma-like sleep because I knew I had a big day coming on that Friday. That was the day my soul would find redemption and true eternal peace.

"When we all got up and arrived at my apartment, we knocked on the door and found out that Sophia wasn't there. My mother called Sophia to find out where she was and Sophia informed my mother that she got her belongings out and would be back after the family leaves. So my mother told me to change the cylinder on my door; this way Sophia Cruz would be locked out.

"After the family cleared out, I did everything that needed to be done. I was in such a happy place. A week later I was tickled pink when Sophia came back but couldn't get in because she no longer had the correct keys. She banged on my door for hours, cursing and yelling till the police came and escorted her out of the building and away from my life."

John takes a deep breath and says, "God was truly on my side and I'm truly blessed to be free from this emotional pitfall and thankful for my mother and sister." John looks Edward in the eyes and says "Thank you, brother, for listening to my story and always pushing me in the right direction." The two men shake and part ways with a much better understanding and a genuine profound level of sincere respect.

Chapter Six
Reminiscing

Edward and his mother were in the kitchen reminiscing about recent and past family gatherings and events. Cleopatra smiles at Edward and asked him if he remembered his thirty-first birthday party at Aunt Viola's house and how his aunt Tierra came up in there crying like a little bitch because their brother Tony was banned from the party for his countless acts of selfishness and shadiness. Edward answers yes, while slightly giggling. "Tierra was a hot mess and neglected to tell us that she spoke to Tony the night before and told him if he couldn't come then she and her family wouldn't show up either," he said.

"We all knew she was just blowing smoke up your brother's ass," said Edward, "but the sad thing is he actually believed your sister Minister Tierra Joy, who is without a doubt the biggest liar and crook who ever walked this Earth with the exception of your mother."

Cleopatra starts talking about how Tierra would nag her repeatedly about Tony to the point she lost her cool and said, "Bitch, what is the matter with you? I'm not feeding your brother or his greedy-ass girlfriend, so leave me the fuck alone and stop trying to hustle me. Better yet, did you prepare that tuna fish salad for my baby's birthday party?" Tierra says no. Cleopatra tells her sister, "Get the fuck away from me and make that damn salad, you freeloading, greedy bitch. And if that salad isn't done, I'm going to slap your trifling, high, yellow ass to sleep."

Well, needless to say, Tierra did the right thing and got out of dodge because she and her family were skating on really thin ice themselves.

Edward and his mother laughed for a while when Marcus Sr. joined in the conversation: "Hey, what about when Tierra decided to be slick and have Mother's Day at Viola's house with Tony, Daisy, Princess, and Lucas but neglected to invite us and your mother? We busted up in there and caught them in the act, and all Tierra could do was stand there and look stupid.

"Meanwhile Tony goes to the car while I'm waiting on Cleopatra and tells me to come in the house and speak to everyone because the family was under the impression that I was mad at them. And when I came in the house, Cleopatra tore me a new one for leaving her valuables in the car so far away from the house. And after she was done with me she literally put a hurting on Tony so bad he just sat down and started crying like a newborn baby getting his ass popped for the very first time.

"But when Tierra came in the house after being in the backyard grilling food, she saw him crying and asked everyone what was wrong. Her husband said he pissed off Cleopatra but before Lucas could finish the rest of his statement, Tierra just threw her hands in the air and went back outside with the food."

The Jones family was really entertained by the ongoing stories and chatter when Edward also remembered one incident when the Jones family went to Brooklyn, NY to attend Viola's family and friends' boat ride. Everyone was having a nice time until Lillian wanted to sit with the Jones family and Viola and Tony; however, there was no room for her. She asked her oldest child and only son Tony if he could move over so she could join them and Tony's reply was "I'd rather eat shit and die, you scarecrow-looking bitch." Lillian answered, "Well, fuck you, you half-dead motherfucker. That's why your son can't stand you and why no one in this family respects your stupid, dumb ass, especially since you're living with a bitch who doesn't do shit but suck dick and eat all the time."

Tony just rolled his eyes and said nothing; eventually Lillian asked Marcus Sr. if he would be willing to move over so she could sit and of course he did. And by him doing so, Tony just got up from his seat and proceeded to find another place to rest and relax. Lillian starts to call her son back, but he looks back at her and tells her, "Drop dead already, and do us all a favor, you stink-ass, bottom-of-the-barrel, gutter bitch."

Well, it's safe to assume that the Jones family has some very entertaining stories, and everyone in the Jones family has no trouble telling the stories well, especially since none of them was made up, and everything is better than any movie or television script.

Chapter Seven
Ongoing Drama

Viola and Cleopatra were on the phone having their usual conversation when Viola asked Cleopatra if she knew about their cousin Raymond Fraud's retirement party he was having in a few days in Glen Clove, TX. Tierra Joy, her family, and their brother Tony were all invited to the event. Viola had just decided she was going as well since Raymond's sister Gina made it her prime business to invite Viola, mainly because she was hoping that the offer would get her another big bag of baby stuff similar to what she had gotten for her first grandbaby who was a little cutie. Cleopatra tells Viola that neither Tierra nor their brother Tony told her anything, and she hasn't heard from Raymond or Gina because they were still mad at the fact that they couldn't bring their large family to New York City for the Jones family retirement party for Marcus Sr.; the Jones family was on a tight budget and couldn't handle over forty-five family members from Glen Clove, plus friends of the Jones family, Marcus Sr.'s rather large family, and Tierra's three hundred and forty six people she invited from churches, congregations, and synagogues all over.

The truth is, Cleopatra and her family were being isolated, and it really was a blessing because their family actions gave them just what they needed—a piece of mind and financial stability because now the Jones family was free of any burden or typical shady family tactics.

Cleopatra asked her sister if their cousin Gina ever called and thanked her for those two rather large baby bags she had received, and Viola said no she never said a word and guessed Gina was waiting to see what kind of stuff her second grandbaby gets.

Viola and Cleopatra continued talking while Viola got ready for her siblings to come pick her up and make their way to Glen Clove. Once Tierra arrived at Viola's and rang her phone, Cleopatra wished her younger sister well and told her to be safe and keep those money-hungry Negros' hands out of your pocket. Viola laughs and promises to do just that and tells Cleopatra she loves her and hangs up.

But it wouldn't be the last conversation the two sisters would have because when Viola and her other siblings arrived in Glen Clove, TX, it was truly an experience Viola McBride would never forget.

Chapter Eight
A Crying Damn Shame

Cleopatra and Edward were sitting down talking in their apartment when Viola rings Cleopatra's phone and begins to tell her about their cousin Raymond's retirement party, and how Gina's oldest son who had the cute little girl was acting all snotty and rude towards her along with his baby mama whom Viola referred to as a "lost and uneducated soul who needs some all-around spiritual healing and redemption."

Apparently Tierra and running buddy Lyla were whispering lies and hate in the ears of Gina's oldest son and his woman, and that's why the couple's attitude toward Viola was funky and rude.

But back to the story, Viola tells Cleopatra that the party was pure ghetto trash. They had very little food and a massive turn-out mainly because Raymond invited family, friends, and even strangers on Facebook, which didn't make sense since he already had a load of greedy Negros who came with nothing but big mouths and even bigger appetites.

In short, the food was devoured within ten or fifteen minutes and most of the guests were so drunk they couldn't go home. As a result, they pretty much all slept over Raymond's house like it was a college campus hangout spot.

Viola was so disgusted by everything she had seen she decided to leave a day early and took the bus back. This way she could have peace of mind and, more importantly, wouldn't have to worry about her sister and brother-in-law trying to rip her off going back home the way they did on the way down. Everyone was supposed to chip in for the gas and tolls on their way to the event. Needless to say, Viola was happy to be home and told her sister that she was right, and she should have stayed home because the experience was a disaster that didn't make any damn sense.

Chapter Nine
The Phone Conversation

Edward was walking out the door taking the trash to the dump site when he decided to give his uncle Tony a phone call; a few weeks back Tony and Cleopatra got into a verbal altercation at his aunt Viola's house, and Edward wanted to know what was said and why his uncle made it a point to upset his mother.

So Edward rings his uncle's phone and says, "Hey, Uncle Tony, it's your nephew Edward. I'm calling because my mother is still a little agitated about your fight, and I want to know what happened because her blood pressure is kind of high."

The next thing he knew, his uncle starts yelling and screaming at him like he's a certified gangster, and this is how the conversation between the two started off. Tony gets real loud and ignorant with Edward and says, "Look, you four-eyed nigger, you don't question me about your mother's and my situation, you simple motherfucker."

At this point Edward loses his cool. He called his uncle Tony very calmly and respectfully, but once Tony stated he wanted to take their problem to a street level, Edward was more than ready to go, responding, "Bitch, who the fuck do you think you're talking to like that, you disrespectful, good-for-nothing, high, yellow son of a bitch. You're not going to talk to me in that tone, you waffle-colored Negro. As a matter of fact, you can kiss my black ass and go to hell, you fucking, crab-in-the-barrel, house nigger."

Tony was overwhelmed but tried to cut his nephew off so he could speak. Edward, however, refused to allow him to say anything else because, at this point, Edward just went into a rage and gave Tony a tongue lashing he never expected. Tony started whimpering like a little puppy, and Daisy just went on ahead and advised Tony to hang up the phone. But, boy, who would have thought Tony McBride would be foolish enough to hang up on someone during mid cursing? But he did and Edward called him back and left a message because his uncle was too scared to take the call. Edward basically said on the voicemail that Tony was dead to him and if he ever saw him again he was going to break his boots in his ass and leave the strings in there.

Now what Tony should have done was leave it alone but, no, he called his sister Tierra and played the voicemail for her. She made a copy of the recording; this way she could replay it over to all the family members from down south, upstate New York, and the rest of the world, especially if they were interested. Edward didn't care because he was trying to find out why his uncle would deliberately try to kill his mother with street ghetto foolishness, but one thing was certain—Tony and Tierra crossed a dangerous line, and if it wasn't for their sister Cleopatra taking the time to calm Edward down, there was a very good chance his aunt and uncle would have found themselves in a bad situation.

Chapter Ten
The Final Story

Edward Jones was sitting at his job reflecting on his life and what he had accomplished while taking into consideration that he never really got the full love and support from a large portion of his family members from neither his mother's nor his father's side. But Edward refused to feel sorry for himself. In fact, he made a decision right then and there that he was going to really make a hard push to promote his newest book project and wasn't going to expect any help from anyone, considering that the supportive track record of most of the people he loves was virtually non-existent.

      Edward Jones was known for being that shy, sensitive boy who never went out of his way to hurt anyone for the most part, but now he believes he has to be more aggressive and assertive, especially if he's going to walk this journey on his own. Edward Jones always believed in his heart that the people he loved overall meant him no harm, but that was a time when his eyes were blinded by one-sided loyalty and ignorance.

But today is a new day, and he is ready for anything and everything because he walks with a much more positive attitude and an even stronger confidence than before. Edward Jones has opened his eyes and can finally see what his mother and Aunt Gladys told him years ago—that not everyone who says they love you genuinely loves you because their actions speak volumes. And that, my friends, was some of the best advice Edward Jones ever received in his lifetime.

In conclusion, this may be the last chapter of this book, but it's definitely not the last story to be told.

CPSIA information can be obtained
at www.ICGtesting.com
Printed in the USA
LVOW10s2010260217

525476LV00001B/111/P